A Christmas Eve Adventure

A Christmas Eve Adventure

FINDING THE LIGHT OF THE WORLD

For information about this title or to order other books and/or electronic media, contact the publisher:

Kathleen Lockwood/Diotima Press
thelightoftheworldbook.com
info@thelightoftheworldbook.com

ISBNs:
978-0-9642128-3-1 (hardcover)
978-0-9642128-1-7 (softcover)
978-0-9642128-2-4 (eBook)

Printed in the United States of America

Cover and Interior design: 1106 Design

A CHRISTMAS EVE ADVENTURE

FINDING THE LIGHT OF THE WORLD

REV. KATHLEEN LOCKWOOD

This book is dedicated to Trieste, Dominick and Amelia Lockwood, my inspiration for these stories.

WHOOSH!

"What was that?" the father yelled as he slammed on the brakes.

"A bird? I almost hit it! What's it doing out here in this snowstorm?"

The children woke up with a jolt and immediately started to fight.

"Cammy took my cookie!" cried Sammy.

"You weren't even eating it!" Cammy declared.

Their sister little Lammy began to cry.

"Let's not fight on the way to your Christmas pageant," scowled their mother. "You've made little Lammy cry!"

Once parked, they made their way toward the church. A dark shape loomed out from between the parked cars. Startled, the family stepped back as a shabbily dressed man held out his hand to them.

"Do you have anything for an old man?" he asked.

Sammy huddled behind his father's legs, and Cammy ignored him.

Jealous that she had not been chosen to play Mary in the
pageant that night, Cammy whispered to her friends,
"I would have been much better than Lindsey!"
Lindsey overheard Cammy and felt a wave
of sadness sweep over her.

Excitement filled the air backstage as their Sunday School teacher helped her students transform sheets and blankets into shepherd costumes.

The pageant was running smoothly until it was time for Sammy to say his line. Gripped by stage fright, he looked at the audience and froze! Everyone looked like monsters to him! Frightened, he ran off the stage, crying.

Later that night, Sammy and Cammy talked about all the presents that Santa was going to bring them. "Do you think Santa brought baby Jesus presents when he was born?" Sammy asked his sister. "I wish I had been there! "Look," he said, "there's Santa now!" Cammy turned toward the window. "That's not Santa," she said. "It's just a star, silly."

"Look! That star is moving closer and closer," Sammy yelled. "It's so close I bet I can touch it!"

He put his hand up to the window, and the glass dissolved!

Suddenly, an angel appeared and grabbed Sammy!

"Help!" he cried out to Cammy as he was pulled out the window.

Flying in the arms of an angel, Sammy
and Cammy passed through space and time.

Sammy and Cammy found themselves lying on the cold, rocky ground of a field.

"What did you do, Sammy?" Cammy yelled. "Where are we? What are we wearing?"

Sammy ignored her when he saw a tiny baby lamb prancing toward them.

"Oh, look," he exclaimed as he reached to pet it. "It's a real baby lamb!"

A voice yelled out, "Leave our sheep alone!" Startled, they turned to see two children running toward them.

A large group of people dressed in the same strange clothes approached them.

"What's going on here?" the leader asked. "Who are you?"

Sammy and Cammy looked at their new clothes, the lambs, and the strangers, and began to cry.

Just then, *WHOOSH!*

A large white dove circled in front of them and flew up into the sky . . .

Everyone's eyes followed the bird, and, as they looked up, they noticed a very bright star moving toward them.

It got bigger and bigger! An angel appeared inside the blinding light!

Everyone ran to hide, but when the angel's musical voice filled the night air, they were comforted.

"Do not be afraid!" she said,

"I am here to bring you news of great joy for all people.

For on this very day, your Savior and King was born in Bethlehem.

And this will be a sign to you; you will find a newborn wrapped in swaddling bands of cloth, lying in a stable."

More angels appeared then, lighting up the sky.
They were singing,

"Glory to God, the Most High.
Peace upon the Earth,
and good will for all people."

When all the
angels began to fly
back into the night,
Sammy forgot his
shyness and ran up
to the first angel.

"Wait! Wait!" he cried
in desperation. "Where are
we? Why are we here?"

Cammy chimed in, "And
how do we get home?"

The angel smiled kindly at the two
frightened children. "You have traveled back in
time to the first Christmas!
Don't cry—you will go home as
soon as you discover why you
are here," she said mysteriously.

And then, *POOF!* She
was gone.

Happily, the shepherds started off toward Bethlehem, singing and chatting excitedly.

"This is great!" Sammy declared. "I'm going to tell them all about Jesus."

He tugged at the leader's sleeve and said, "The baby we are looking for is, '*Caaa, Caaa, Caaa!!*'"

"What language is that?" asked the shepherd.

Frustrated, Sammy ran away in tears as everyone continued their walk.

Cammy laughed so hard she had to stop to catch her breath.

"What were you telling them about Jesus? Oh, I know, '*Caaa, Caaa, Caaa.*'"

She pointed to the bird circling over them. "That bird can tell them more about Jesus than you can," she laughed.

WHOOSH!

The bird landed on Sammy's shoulder! "Well, yes, I can," it said, "but I won't."

"What?" they both exclaimed in unison, "*a talking bird!?!*"

The bird continued, "They hear you talking in their language now, *but*, if you try to tell them about the future, you will sound just like me."

With that, the bird flew off. "*Caaa, Caaa, Caaa!*"

The group arrived in Bethlehem, just as the town was waking up.

"Good morning," a shepherd said to a woman feeding animals in her front yard. "We are looking for a newborn king."

"King?" the woman laughed. "There's no king here!"

They walked through the town, looking into stables and asking the same questions over and over again. They saw babies wrapped in fine silk and babies in cradles, but they did not see a newborn baby in a stable wrapped in a simple cloth.

By the end of the day, everyone was exhausted.

"That angel must have been a dream!" one shepherd said. "There's no king here."

"We need to go home!" chimed in another.

Sammy panicked. "We can't go back! He's here, somewhere!"

Suddenly, *WHOOSH!*

The bird landed on his shoulder.

"Birdie," he said, "can you help us find Jesus?"

"You only needed to ask," answered the bird. "Follow me!"

Cammy yelled to the sleepy shepherds, "Come on! We know where to go!"

"We've already looked everywhere," the leader said with despair. "It's time to go home."

"But we have a guide now!" called Cammy as they ran off after the bird. "Come on, everyone! Let's find the newborn king!"

One by one, the shepherds shrugged, got up, and followed them.

They followed the bird all the way to a house at the far edge of town. Then they scrambled down the hill toward the stable.

There, they turned the corner and . . .

"Oh, my!" said Cammy.

"It's Jesus!" cried Sammy. "Look! He really *is* the Light of the World!"

"Look, His blanket fell off," Sammy whispered. "Baby Jesus must be cold, but what can we do? He's God. Do we dare to go near Him?" A tear dropped down his face.

"I think so," answered his sister, softly. "Jesus was born to help us get closer to God. Let's cover him up together."

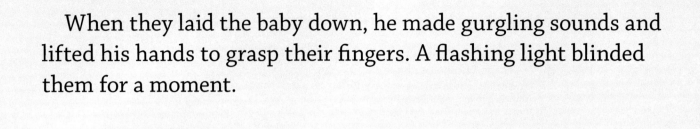

When they laid the baby down, he made gurgling sounds and lifted his hands to grasp their fingers. A flashing light blinded them for a moment.

When the light died down, they looked at each other and were amazed at what they saw—their own hearts were shining!

They looked around and saw that *everyone* had a glow coming from their hearts!

Just then, the angel reappeared, smiling at the children. "Why do you look so surprised?" she asked. "You know that God is everywhere."

Cammy responded, "Yes, God is everywhere, but I never thought that meant in *me*." She looked around. "And in everyone. What about *mean* people?" she whispered.

The angel smiled. "Sometimes, people can be mean when they forget the light they have inside, but God is still there. Just remember: The greater your love, the brighter your light!"

Just then, "*Caaa! Caaa! Caaa!*" The bird flew down from the rafters. "I think they are ready to go home," she said.

"I miss my mommy and daddy, and little Lammy," said Sammy.

"Me, too," agreed Cammy. "But can we kiss Jesus goodbye?"

"There are no goodbyes," the angel answered. "Jesus will always be in your heart."

As Cammy and Sammy held Jesus in their arms and kissed him, their bodies slowly dissolved into tiny balls of light, and then . . .

WHOOSH!
"What was that? A bird?" the father yelled as he slammed on the brakes.
"I almost hit it! What's it doing out here in this snowstorm?"
The children napping in the back seat woke up with a jolt.
Cammy and Sammy laughed about how much fun a snow day would be as their Mom passed out cookies.

Once parked, they made their way toward the church. A shabbily dressed man held out his hand to them.

"Do you have anything for an old man?" he asked.

Cammy stepped up. "Please come inside," she said. "It's warm, and there will be plenty of food."

Happily, the man followed the family into the church.

Excitement filled the air backstage as their Sunday School teacher helped her students transform sheets and blankets into shepherd costumes.

"Lindsey is going to be a great Mary," Cammy told her friends. "She memorized her lines beautifully!"

Lindsey overheard Cammy and smiled.

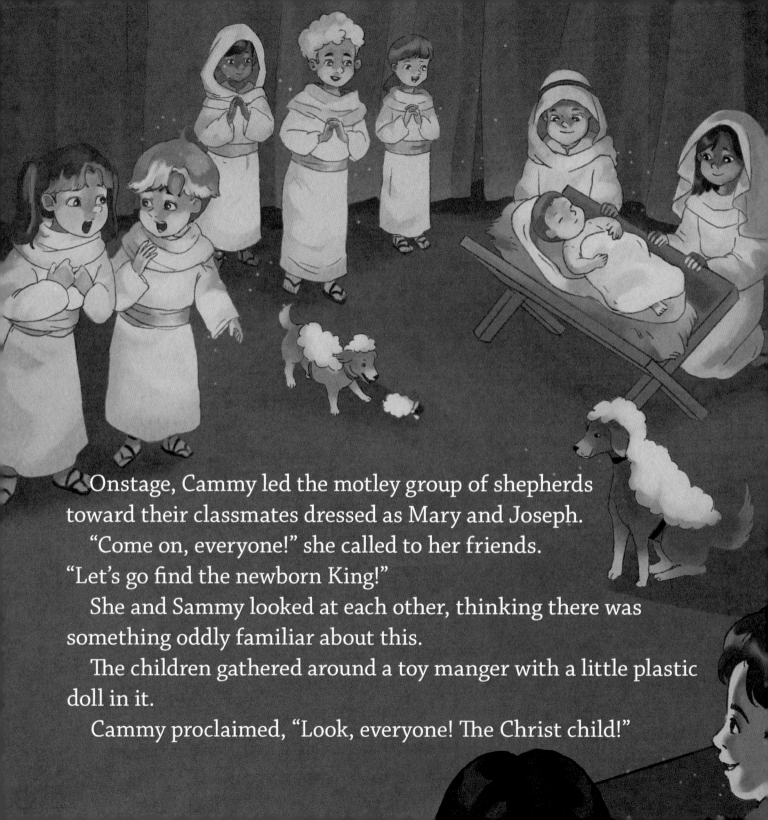

Onstage, Cammy led the motley group of shepherds toward their classmates dressed as Mary and Joseph.

"Come on, everyone!" she called to her friends. "Let's go find the newborn King!"

She and Sammy looked at each other, thinking there was something oddly familiar about this.

The children gathered around a toy manger with a little plastic doll in it.

Cammy proclaimed, "Look, everyone! The Christ child!"

It was time for Sammy to say his line. He looked out at the audience. He saw his parents and many other people smiling. Sammy called out, "Behold the Light of the World!"

Backstage, a hand flipped a switch and the baby doll lit up.
Sammy and Cammy looked at each other, and the glowing baby
doll. Memories of their journey came back to them and they saw
their hearts glowing again! "Oh, my goodness!" Cammy called out.
"I remember!" Sammy answered.

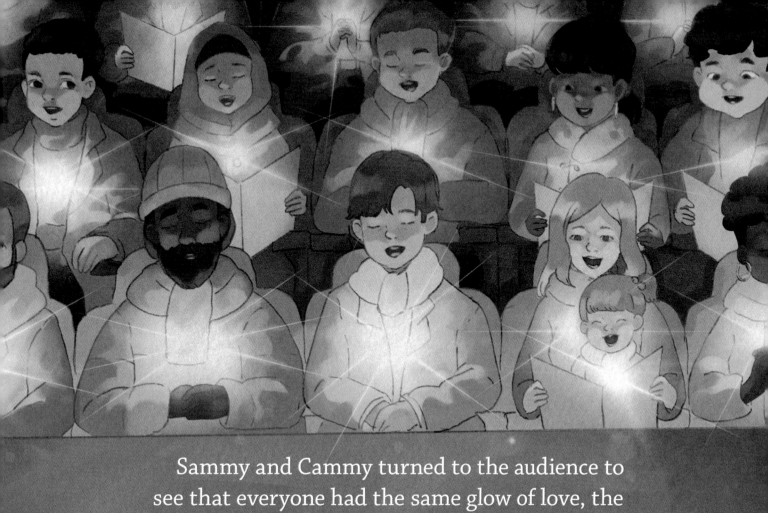

Sammy and Cammy turned to the audience to
see that everyone had the same glow of love, the
light of Christ in their hearts!

Onstage, the children's chorus started to sing,
and the audience joined in:

"Joy to the world/the Lord has come . . ."

Thank you for reading and sharing this. I hope you enjoyed it, found it heartwarming, and that it facilitated a conversation with you and your children.

You might be interested and a brief backstory about what motivated me to write this book.

When I was a child, I was taught that God is everywhere. It is a true and beautiful teaching, but the implication was that God was everywhere "out there." Later I experienced God as an indwelling Spirit, and this powerful lesson opened my heart.

Sammy and Cammy were also changed when they were taken back in time to help the shepherds find Jesus. Once there, Jesus shows them the Divine light within, which opens their eyes to see the same Divine light in everyone, regardless of race or creed.

I believe this empowering teaching of Christ will lead us to true world peace . . .

Online reviews validate that our work matters and my publisher tells me that favorable five-star reviews are the number one reason people decide to buy a book. Please take a few minutes to share what the book meant to you and your children. It would mean a lot.

Please know how much I appreciate that, and I hope this book has an enduringly positive impact on you and your loved ones.

About the Author

Kathleen often entertained her three young children with Sammy, Cammy, and Lammy adventure tales during long car rides. They were pleased to be the inspiration for these stories and always asked for more.

Rev. Lockwood is an Interfaith Minister and the founder of the Heart Self Speaks Collective, a virtual home for those on spiritual journeys. She is the author of the children's book *Amy Angel Goes Home: A Heavenly Tale of Adoption*.

You can find her in the Pocono Mountains meditating or sipping coffee with her poodle, Monet, at her side. Please visit her online at www.theheartselfspeaks.com.

About the Artists

Puteri Esther is an Art Director based in Indonesia, specializing in Illustration. For more information, visit www.puteriesther.com

Winda Kartika Laoli is an Indonesian illustrator, currently an Art and Design student at Bandung Institute of Technology. For more information, visit her Instagram on @kuasbiru.

Ade Chintya is an Indonesia-based illustrator and member of the Society of Children's Book Writers and Illustrators. She has been creating illustrations for children's books since 2016. Her illustrations have been published in a wide variety of print and web media. For more information, visit www.adechint.com

Made in the USA
Middletown, DE
23 December 2021

56945951R00024